HAIRCUT HAZARDS

SIT, STAY, SLEEP COZY MYSTERIES
BOOK 13

PATTI BENNING

SUMMER PRESCOTT BOOKS PUBLISHING

Copyright 2025 Summer Prescott Books

All Rights Reserved. No part of this publication nor any of the information herein may be quoted from, nor reproduced, in any form, including but not limited to: printing, scanning, photocopying, or any other printed, digital, or audio formats, without prior express written consent of the copyright holder.

**This book is a work of fiction. Any similarities to persons, living or dead, places of business, or situations past or present, is completely unintentional.

CHAPTER ONE

Something was wrong. Sadie Barton re-counted the dogs in their kennels. From little Petunia, the Yorkshire Terrier, on one end to Jasper, her own happy-go-lucky foxhound who she was pretty sure had rocks for brains on the other, every one of her canine guests were standing at their chain-link doors, watching her.

Each of them but one.

"Angus," she muttered, narrowing her eyes.

She opened his kennel, where his dog bed, his favorite toy, and a fresh bowl of cold water waited, untouched. She called his name, then to be sure, got on her hands and knees and pushed the dog door flap aside so she could see into the outdoor run. It was empty, and the pea stones were still neatly raked, with no sign of paws messing them up. Much to her relief, the chain-link gate to the outdoor run was shut, and the padlock was still engaged.

"Darn it, Cody." She got to her feet and backed out of the kennel. "Sorry guys, I'll be back to clean in a few minutes. It looks like poor Mr. Angus was dognapped."

She slipped out of the kennel room and made her way to the lobby, unworried. She was ninety-nine percent sure she knew where the missing border collie was, and it was a non-issue… or it would have been if the person who took him had remembered to tell her.

She strode through the laundry room, where both of their industrial-sized washing machines were already hard at work cleaning linens and dog beds, then pushed the next door open and stepped into the lobby. Penelope Montgomery, her best friend and business partner, was hunched over the front desk scribbling furiously on a legal pad. She didn't look up until Sadie was standing right next to the desk. When she did, she jumped slightly and put her pen down.

"How long have you been standing there?"

"For the past hour," Sadie joked. "You didn't even notice when I brought my breakfast down and ate it right next to you."

Her friend rolled her eyes. "Yeah, right. What's up?"

"Can you let me know as soon as you see Cody? I want to talk to him."

"Sure," her friend said, her expression curious. "Oh, I forgot to tell you, he stopped by yesterday evening to pick up Angus. I think you had already gone upstairs for the night. I guess his mom is out of town on another business trip. You know, you really should just let the poor kid adopt that dog."

Sadie's irritation vanished. Cody *had* told someone he was taking Angus home with him. It wasn't his fault Penny had forgotten to tell her.

She acknowledged her friend's suggestion with a sigh. "I know he loves Angus," she said, "but he still lives with his mom and she doesn't want a dog. He's so young, not even nineteen yet. Who knows where he'll be in five years, or even six months? I don't want to put Angus in a position where he's just going to be rehomed again."

"Weren't you eighteen when you got Nova?" Penny asked, naming Sadie's first dog – well, her first personal dog that hadn't been a family dog.

Sadie felt a pang at the thought of the sweet dog who had spent twelve good years with her. She hadn't even been able to even think about getting another dog for a year after she passed. When she was finally ready, she walked into an animal shelter and fell in love with Jasper. The goofy, oblivious, social-butterfly of a foxhound couldn't have been more different than Nova, but he had claimed her heart nonetheless.

"That's different," she said. "I already knew then that I wanted to spend my life working with dogs, and I had my parents' support. I knew if I had to move back home, I would be able to bring her with me."

Penny crossed her arms and raised her eyebrows. "Cody wants to spend *his* life working with dogs, doesn't he? You can't say he doesn't know what he wants because he's so young, because you were the same age when you made that decision. And he may not have parental support, but he's got us – unless you're saying you wouldn't take Angus back or watch him for a while if Cody needed you to."

Sadie didn't have an argument for that, but there was another concern on her mind. "I really want Angus to go somewhere where he'll have a job to do, though. Whether that's herding or sports, he needs something to keep him occupied. A lot of his behavior issues stem from boredom. He's such a smart dog, and I want him to go somewhere that his smarts will excel rather than get him into trouble."

"I mean, Cody might not have a sheep farm, but do you really think he would keep Angus locked up in a crate all day? If he's serious about being a dog trainer — and he seems to be, from what I've heard — then Angus would be a great demo dog, like Jasper is for you. And I'm sure he'd love doing dog sports and stuff."

"Yeah, but there's nowhere around here to *do* sports," Sadie said. "I think the closest place that offers good agility classes is all the way in Atlanta."

Penny stared at her as if she was dense. "We have ten acres of land, and a professional dog trainer whose boyfriend would jump at the chance to build her a dog agility course. And before you say we can't afford it, we're getting close. That's what I've been so busy with all morning; trying to figure out what we should invest in next, since we're finally making a decent profit even with paying Cody and Maria and drawing livable salaries ourselves."

"I didn't realize we were doing so well," Sadie said.

While they were both involved in all aspects of the business, Penny was the one who had taken marketing and business finance courses in college, so those aspects of running Sit, Stay, Sleep naturally fell more to her. Sadie knew the business had been doing better lately, and they were no longer in danger of needing to sell the place, but she hadn't run the numbers in the same way Penny had.

"Well, we are," Penny said. "I don't want to commit to anything major like expanding the rooms or the kennels, but I think we could afford to add some more amenities to the grounds. There are a few things I've been wanting to do to make the motel look more inviting: installing more flower beds, and maybe some bushes or small trees, and paying Sam to add us to his regular rotation so the exterior looks nice consistently are what I want to start with. I'll handle talking to him about money and payment, since I know it's probably kind of weird for you to do since the two of you are dating. I was also thinking we could clean up those trails out back and offer them as an amenity on our website. There were a few things I wanted to get your opinion on, like whether we should build a fenced potty and exercise area for the guests' dogs, and of course we'd set aside funds for your side of the business. I don't know enough about all of that to know what would be the most useful to you right now."

"We need to sit down together and go over all of this," Sadie said. "I haven't even begun to think about a lot of this."

"Yeah, we do," Penny said. "As soon as we both

have time." She glanced at the clock on the wall. "You still have that meeting with the dog groomer at ten, right? Maybe we could talk over lunch."

"Shoot, I almost forgot," Sadie said. She glanced at the clock, too. It was only just after eight, but she still needed to clean the kennels, feed the dogs, and do a short training session with a lab puppy whose owners wanted her to keep up with the dog's manners and obedience while they were gone. She needed to hurry if she wanted to have time to change before the meeting. "Lunch sounds good, but I'd better get back to work for now."

She went back into the kennel, her mind a whirlwind of ideas for the future. Some of her dreams for the motel were finally within reach… starting with her upcoming interview with the woman she hoped would be the newest addition to their team.

CHAPTER TWO

Sadie got done with her chores in the nick of time. She came down from her apartment freshly showered and changed, with Jasper by her side, to see a woman who must be Allison already speaking to Penny.

She looked up when Sadie and Jasper entered the room and gave Sadie a fleeting smile, then immediately turned her attention to Jasper.

"Oh, who's this handsome fellow?" she asked.

The foxhound trotted over to her, his tail wagging as he sniffed her shoes and jeans, and then leaned against her while she scratched at the base of his tail. His mouth was open and his tongue lolled out the side — he looked like he was in heaven.

With any other dog, Sadie would have taken this as a sign that Allison was probably a decent person, but Jasper had never met a stranger in his life. Well, now that she thought about it, there was one person who he didn't like: Garrick Washington, even though that man had saved her life. Jasper, she suspected, simply wasn't a good judge of people... but anyone who liked *him* was all right, in her book.

"So sorry," the stranger said with a laugh as she straightened up. "I love dogs, but he's not the one interviewing me." She extended her hand. "I'm Allison Mason. Thank you so much for agreeing to see me."

The woman looked like she was a little older than her and Penny, with brown hair drawn back into a sensible ponytail and hazel eyes. Sadie shook her hand and introduced herself, then said, "Of course. I have to admit, from what you said in your email, it sounds like there's very little downside for us."

"That's my intention," Allison said as her hand fell back to her side. "I'm hoping we can work out a deal that feels great to both of us. I've been following you guys since you first opened last year, and I would love to be a part of what you're building."

"Unfortunately, we don't have an office that we can use for the interview, so we'll start in here and then I can take you on a tour of the kennels in a little bit," Sadie said. "Feel free to take a seat in one of the chairs, but fair warning – they're not very comfortable. Oh, and if you'd like a cookie from Sunshine Desserts, we have some in the display case in the back corner. You're welcome to take one. We also have some bottled water if you're thirsty."

"I'm fine for now, thank you," Allison said. She sat down on one of the uncomfortable chairs and gave Sadie a look that was both nervous and hopeful. Sadie sat down two seats away from her, with Jasper between them, still begging for attention from Allison, who scratched behind his ears.

This was the first real interview Sadie had given. Penny was the one who had handled hiring Maria, their housekeeper who came two days a week, and Cody didn't have any work experience before they hired him. She felt like she was playing a role that she hadn't earned, but there was nothing to do but begin.

"So, Allison, how long have you been a groomer? And where did you work before this?"

"I've been grooming for… let's see, it'll be a decade this year," Allison said. "For the first three years I worked for a chain pet store. After that, I was a mobile groomer up until just a few months ago. That worked really well for me, and I would love to get back into it at some point, but unfortunately, I lost my trailer and my truck in a fire." Seeing the look on

Sadie's face, she quickly added, "No animals were hurt, I was already home for the evening, and neither vehicle was in use. Still, it was a major blow and my insurance is fighting me on the payout. I did manage to purchase another trailer, but its smaller then what I had before, and I've had to slowly begin building it out myself. Right now, it's pretty much just a shell with rubber flooring and a few outlets, lighting, and water connections installed. I'm keeping an eye out for some used equipment at a decent price. I'm hoping I'll be able to purchase some soon."

"We have a good-sized tub and grooming table in the back," Sadie said. "If this goes well, you'd be welcome to use those until you get your own."

"That would be great," Allison said, perking up. "All I would need to get is a forced air dryer, and I think I actually know someone I can borrow one from, so that means I could start pretty much right away."

"What else would you need to set up here?" Sadie asked.

"Just a place to park and an outlet and hose connection that I can hook the trailer up to. I've been looking into contracts some other groomers use, and what I think would be most fair to both of us is if I pay you a small flat fee each month that would help cover the use of the space, the electricity, and the water, and then you'd also get a percentage of each groom that I do. That way, it wouldn't cost you anything to have me here, and it would be sustainable for me. I won't be trapped into paying a substantial fee each month while I'm still building my client base back up."

That sounded good to Sadie. She struggled to think of a downside, but she couldn't. As long as Allison seemed to know what she was doing and her references checked out, this seemed like an opportunity they needed to jump on.

"Let's start the tour," she suggested, standing up. "I'll show you the facilities and the grooming tub and table I mentioned, and we can chat some more as we walk."

She gave Allison a tour of the kennels, pausing to put Jasper in his kennel next to Angus, who had been safely returned when Cody arrived earlier that morning. Their young employee was currently outside pulling weeds around the dog runs, and they had come to an agreement that he could take Angus home after work for the rest of the week. She had been thinking about what Penny said that morning, and had decided that she would be okay with Cody adopting Angus, if only he had his own place… or at least lived with a parent who actually wanted a dog in the house.

After touring the inside of the building, they went outside so Allison could look for a good place to hook the grooming table up. There was an outdoor outlet on the left side of the building, not too far from a hose spigot. Allison would need to install a water heater in her trailer, but Sadie thought they would be able to work out a deal where they bought one for her and she paid them back over time. She couldn't imagine losing everything in a fire and not even having an insurance payout to help start over, and wasn't opposed to helping Allison get back on her feet as long as they at least came out even in the end.

By the time they returned to the lobby, she had all but decided to hire Allison. All that was left to do was check the references Allison had given her and do a little more research on her own to make sure she was hiring someone with a good reputation. The most important thing was that whoever she hired would treat the dogs well. That was one thing she wouldn't give any second chances on.

She was hoping Penny would get a chance to ask Allison some questions of her own, but her friend was busy helping a guest when they got back to the lobby. She walked Allison over to the cookie display and encouraged the other woman to take one on the house. They waited there, hoping the issue the guest was having would be resolved quickly. Sadie tuned in and tried to figure out what the conversation was about.

The guest looked like she was in her thirties, with coiffed brown hair that fell to her shoulders and a ridiculous amount of eyeliner... and she looked livid.

"So, you're saying you're not going offer me any solutions?"

"I'm not sure what you want me to do," Penny said.

"I want you to get someone to deliver my food to me," the woman said. "This is ridiculous. I've already bought and paid for it."

"We don't offer that service," Penny said. "I already told you, you're going to have to use a proper delivery service."

"None of them will deliver it from Burns," she complained. "They'll say it's 'too far.'"

"In that case, you'll have to go get the food yourself."

"That would take almost an hour of driving if I went there and back," the woman said. "I don't have time for that."

Penny looked utterly exasperated. "I'm afraid I

don't either, ma'am. I suggest calling the restaurant and seeing if you can cancel your order."

"But there isn't anywhere else that sells seafood in the area."

Allison, standing next to Sadie, shot her an amused look. Sadie's lips twitched as she tried not to look too entertained. It was clear Penny and this woman had been going around in circles for a while.

"Look, ma'am, this is a roadside motel, not a five-star luxury hotel. I'm afraid we can't help you."

"Can't or won't?" the woman snapped. She turned to go, then spun and pointed her finger at Penny. "I'm going to be leaving a *very* negative review about this. What happened to 'the customer is always right'? I'm sick of being treated like I'm the problem when in reality, customer service has been going downhill for years."

She stomped out of the lobby. Penny collapsed into the rolling chair behind the front desk with a groan, and Sadie finally approached with Allison.

"That was a new one," she said, grinning.

"That woman is insane," Penny grumbled. "Worse, she's staying here all week. What's she going to complain about next? That we don't have a cheese and wine selection tucked away in some fancy cellar?" She rolled her eyes, then sat up a little straighter and smiled at Allison. "Sorry about that. What did you think of the tour?" She leaned forward, her expression turning predatory. "And how would you feel about offering discounts to our guests' dogs during their stay here?"

CHAPTER THREE

After a little more research and a final discussion with Penny, they decided to sign the contract with Allison, who wouldn't be an employee, but a separate business that contracted space from them.

She started work that Thursday, after having a boxy white trailer towed to the hotel. She had already applied decals advertising *Allison's Pet Grooming* to the sides, but it was clear that the trailer had been bought secondhand and was a work in progress.

Sadie spent a busy Thursday helping Allison put the finishing touches on the trailer. Sam came over to help them install the water heater, and Allison had borrowed a professional-grade forced air dryer from her friend. By the time they finished, the trailer looked professional, if a little bare bones.

"Thankfully I'm in the habit of bringing most of my tools inside with me, so all of my good combs and scissors and trimmers are fine," Allison said as she organized her items. She looked around and gave a pleased sigh. "It feels great to have a place to work again."

Sadie smiled at the other woman. "Welcome aboard. I think this is going to work out great for both of us – and the dogs, too."

Allison didn't get any grooming clients that first day besides Jasper — she volunteered to wash him, and Sadie was happy to sit back and watch someone else scrub the dust and dirt from her dog's coat for once. Mud was like a magnet for him, and every time it rained he somehow made a mud bath out of his outdoor runs, despite the thick layer of pea stones she had laid down.

Penny put her art skills to good use, and helped Allison draw a sign on a chalkboard stand, advertising ten-dollar walk-in nail trims for dogs and cats, which they set up near the road.

The first client arrived on Friday, and by the time the weekend was over, Sadie and Penny were both thrilled with the newest addition to the motel. Not only did they get a small percentage of the profits from each groom, but Allison's dog grooming trailer brought a lot more people to the motel, which was essentially free advertising for them.

Better yet, they had already gotten some new clients through her. Allison had reached out to some of her favorite clients to invite them to her new location, and two of them had already scheduled future boarding or training classes with Sadie, while quite a few of the regulars at the boarding kennel were interested in Allison's professional grooming services… especially since Penny had worked out a deal where guests' dogs and boarding clients got a discount on grooming during their stays.

Allison fit in well with their employees, too. Cody just liked having another dog person around and had already asked Allison for tips on keeping Angus' long coat neatly groomed, and Maria seemed to enjoy having someone a little closer to her age around to chat with when she took her break.

All in all, it felt almost *too* good to be true. Sadie was still waiting for the other shoe to drop.

Lunchtime on Friday, a week after Allison joined them, Sadie found herself covering for Penny in the lobby while her friend went out to pick up some takeout for lunch. Celebrating Fridays was a hard habit to break, even though the day no longer signaled the end of the week for them. Both of them worked seven days a week, and probably would for the foreseeable future. At least Maria and Cody took *some* of the pressure off, and that meant they could occasionally go out together for a meal or some shopping.

Today wasn't one of those days, though. Cody was walking some of the boarding dogs, a job Sadie trusted him with after over a month of training and watching him work with the dogs, and while Maria was here, she only handled cleaning the rooms. Sadie didn't mind, though. She had her own project she was working on: deciding what addition she wanted to make to the dog side of the business that would fall within the budget plan she and Penny had agreed upon. It felt dangerous, spending so much of what they had managed to save, but she knew it was important to pour most of their profits back into the business, especially during the first couple of years.

She was in the middle of wondering if they had enough flat space between the motel and the tree line to clear and grade a multi-purpose field for outdoor dog activities, without the added expense of removing trees and stumps, when the lobby door opened and a middle-aged red-haired woman came in. She had a gorgeous fluffy white Samoyed on a leash beside her.

"Hi," Sadie said with a smile. "Welcome. How can I help you?"

She surreptitiously clicked out of the notes she had been making on the laptop and opened their scheduling program. She didn't remember seeing any appointments for boarding or grooming at this time, but it was possible she had missed something, or someone else had added one and she hadn't seen the notification.

Nope. Lunch was still blocked off for everyone except Cody, who was in the system since he assisted her during her group lessons sometimes.

"Hi," the woman said cheerfully. "I'm Georgia McKinney. And yes, I've heard it all before, and no, I wasn't born in Georgia. I heard that Allison Mason is working here now? I saw her grooming trailer outside when I pulled in. I was hoping I could book something for Kiana over the weekend, or even today if she has time."

"Sure, I can get you booked in," Sadie said. She filtered the scheduling program so she could see just Allison's open blocks. She set the times she was available herself, then any one of them could add appointments to the schedule for those times, and she would get a notification. It was a handy system. "It looks like she has an open appointment at one tomorrow, and then she has quite a few available times on Monday."

"Let's do tomorrow," Georgia said. "I want to do the full wash and trim package, all the works. She knows exactly how I like Kiana to look."

"Got it," Sadie said. She recorded Georgia's contact information and the dog's name. "Since we're working with a new system, we'll need you to provide your dog's vaccination record again, and I'll take down any notes you have for her just in case she needs a refresher."

"I'll email you Kiana's vet records," Georgia said. "But I know she'll remember how I like her to be groomed. I was one of her best clients before that horrible accident. Can you tell me if the discount still applies?"

"I'll have to ask her about that," Sadie said. As far as she knew, Allison wasn't offering any discounts besides the one for dogs that were staying with them, but it was possible she had something arranged with Georgia prior to the fire. "I've got you in the system now, and I'll ask Allison to give you a call about the rest."

"Thank you so much," Georgia said. "We'll get out of your hair now. Say bye, Kiana."

The Samoyed was too busy sniffing the floor to pay any mind to her owner. Sadie watched the gorgeous dog leave the lobby with her owner, a little jealous. Almost as soon as the lobby door shut, the door to the laundry room opened and Allison peeked out.

"Please tell me I'm hallucinating and that wasn't Georgia McKinney who was sniffing around the motel."

Sadie looked at her curiously. Seeing that the woman and her dog were gone, Allison left the laundry room, but stood poised by the door, as if ready to duck back inside at a moment's notice.

"I just put her down for a Saturday appointment," Sadie said. "Should I call and cancel? I'm sorry, I didn't know there was a negative history between you two."

"Ugh, no, I'll see Kiana. I miss that dog, it'll be nice to groom her again. Georgia's just… a lot." She sighed. "Did she say how she found out I'm here?"

"No, just that she heard you were working here, and she also saw your trailer when she pulled in."

Allison wrinkled her nose. "I shouldn't have bought those decals. Can you do me a favor, and let me know if anyone else asks for me? And I'd rather you don't confirm that I'm working here without talking to me first. I've been careful to only reach out to clients who I trust, but I'm worried about what will happen if the news spreads."

"Well, all right." It was a strange request, but easy enough to agree to. "I've got to ask, though… why?"

Allison hesitated. "Because there's a possibility the fire that destroyed my old grooming trailer and my truck wasn't an accident. I don't know who started it, and I'm afraid of what will happen if they find out where I'm working now."

CHAPTER FOUR

Sadie wanted to know more, but Penny returned with the takeout before she could get answers out of Allison, and the other woman took the chance to make herself scarce. She looked worried, and worse, *scared*, as she hurried away.

"What's wrong?" Penny asked as she took their food out of the bag.

"Allison just told me the fire that destroyed her truck and her grooming trailer might not have been accidental," Sadie said. "And she's been trying to keep her new location quiet."

"Would have been nice if she told us that before we signed a contract with her," Penny said, scowling. "Does she think the motel might be in danger?"

"I don't know. I hope not. I didn't get a chance to ask her anything before she hurried out of here."

The thought of a fire at the motel, especially when there were dogs boarding in the kennels, made her pulse spike. She had to remind herself that the kennel room was made entirely out of cinderblock and concrete, they had more than enough smoke detectors, and she slept right above the laundry and would be able to get all of the dogs out quickly if something went wrong.

Despite her attempts at logic, the anxiety stayed at a low simmer as she opened the box that contained her meal: a chicken salad sandwich and sweet potato fries, both from The Creek Kitchen, the local diner. She had yet to be disappointed by anything she got there, and Penny's Caesar salad wrap looked just as mouthwatering as her sandwich.

"We need to find out more," Penny said as she sat down at the front desk and pulled her food closer to her. "We should both go talk to her once we're done eating."

They tried to do just that, but by the time they finished their meal and went outside to find Allison in her grooming trailer, her trailer was locked up tight, and her tiny hatchback was nowhere to be seen – she was gone. When they returned to the lobby, Sadie checked the schedule to find that Allison had cancelled the rest of her appointments for the day.

"Well, that's not suspicious at all," Penny muttered. "I'm going to call her."

Sadie thought it was unlikely that Allison would answer, as she clearly didn't want to talk, but it was worth a try. Unsurprisingly, the call rang through to voicemail, and when Penny tried a second time, the call was outright rejected.

They shared a worried look.

"She hasn't cancelled tomorrow's appointments," Sadie said, glancing at the computer. "If she comes in, we'll talk to her then and figure out what *exactly* is going on. If she doesn't... well, we'll figure something out."

Penny nodded, and Sadie could tell her friend was just as worried as she was – not just for Allison, but also for the motel and what they were trying to build here. They already had enough problems, they didn't need someone bringing even more trouble right to their doorstep.

Maybe she would have noticed it anyway, or maybe it was because she was still worried about a fire and had subconsciously primed herself to be hyper-aware of unusual smells, but the instant Sadie went down to the lobby with Jasper the next morning, she caught the chemical scent in the air. Immediately on edge, she hurried into the kennel room to check on the boarding dogs. Thankfully, the smell wasn't as strong in there. She put Jasper in his kennel at the far end, but didn't open the sliding doors to the outdoor runs.

"Sorry, guys," she said as she unlocked the back door and prepared to go outside. "You're going to have to hold it for a little longer. I need to figure out what that smell is first."

Her first thought was that someone was spraying chemicals around the motel – pesticide or herbicide – but that didn't make sense. The only person other than herself and Penny to handle the yardwork and lawncare at the motel was Sam, and she knew he wouldn't spray any chemicals around the dogs, even if he used them on some of his other clients' yards.

She left through the kennel room's back door, and as soon as she stepped outside, the smell was both stronger, and easier to identify; paint. More confused than ever – she didn't know why someone would be *painting* on the motel's property – she followed the smell around the building, to the northern side where Allison's grooming trailer was parked.

Allison had returned, and she was... spray painting the sides of her trailer white, covering the decals that had advertised her business's name, phone number, and website.

"What are you doing?"

Allison jumped a little and thankfully stopped spraying the paint before she turned toward Sadie. She gave a nervous laugh when she saw her.

"Sorry, you startled me. I decided the decals weren't a good idea. I got here early to try to take them off before my first client arrives, but the methods I read about online either weren't working or would have taken *forever*, so I decided to do it the quick and easy way. Don't worry, I'm being careful not to get any on the building or the grass."

Sure enough, she had laid cardboard on the grass under where she was currently painting, and seemed to have taken care not to let any of the spray get blown toward the wall next to the trailer. Sadie *was* glad she wasn't getting spray paint all over the motel, but she was more concerned with the reason behind all of this.

"Is this because of yesterday?" she asked. "Because of Georgia? You left before I could clarify anything with you."

Alison sighed, her shoulders drooping. "It's not

because of Georgia specifically. She's… fine. A little 'extra,' but she wouldn't do anything malicious. If anything, she's been *too* friendly ever since I gave her a heads up that her husband was having an affair – long story, and not mine to tell. I'm just worried about what will happen if the wrong person drives past and sees my trailer. It was probably stupid to put the decals on it in the first place, but I was trying to be optimistic. You don't know what it was like, losing almost everything I worked toward in a single day. I just wanted everything to go back to normal as soon as possible."

"What happened, Allison? Really?" Sadie asked. "I just want to know what we're getting involved in. I have a business to protect, too, and not just a building, but the dogs and people who are trusting us to keep them safe while they're here."

"I don't *know* what happened," the other woman insisted. "I thought the fire was an accident at first, maybe an electrical fault or an issue with a battery, but a few weeks ago my insurance told me their investigators determines the fire was set intentionally. I filed a police report, but as far as what actually happened, I have no idea."

"Did you have any other issues with your grooming business before that?"

Allison hesitated. "There were some... weird things. But the fire is the closest I've gotten to actually getting hurt, and I think it was pretty clear to whoever started it that no one was in the trailer at the time. I wouldn't put anyone, humans or dogs, at risk if I thought whoever was behind the fire was out to hurt someone."

Sadie frowned. It seemed like Allison was putting a lot of faith into her guesswork of what the mystery arsonist's intentions were.

"What were the other incidents?" she asked.

Allison checked her watch. "It was nothing major, I promise, but I don't have time to go into details right now. I want to finish this and give the paint time to dry before my first client gets here."

"Fine." She understood Allison not wanting the dogs to be around wet paint, and she couldn't exactly ask her to leave the project half finished, especially if the decals might draw the wrong sort of attention. "But we need to talk today: you, me, and Penny. I think we have a right to know exactly what's going on."

"That's fair," Allison said. "I should be free from noon to one. Do you want to talk during lunch?"

"I have a lunch date," Sadie said. "It'll have to be

later in the afternoon. After four, probably, because I have a private training session at two."

Allison agreed to keep some time free that evening, and Sadie promised to let Penny know. She didn't like letting it wait for so long, but Allison had already been working here for a week, so she figured a few more hours couldn't hurt too much. She didn't want to have to ask the other woman to leave and end their contract with her, but she also didn't want to expose their guests or their canine clients to any extra risks.

She returned to the kennel room and finally let the boarding dogs and Jasper out into their runs, then began her morning chores: cleaning, feeding, and dispersing medicine to the dogs that needed it. By the time she finished, the rest of the motel had truly woken up. Maria was busy cleaning rooms, Penny was practically tearing her hair out at the computer trying to fix an error in their latest advertising campaign, and Allison was busy with her grooming clients. Saturdays were one of their busiest days, which left Sadie little time to think about the problems Allison might have brought with her.

Dogs were being picked up and dropped off left and right, and Sadie barely had the time to go upstairs and change into something halfway decent after their morning drop-off hours ended. By the time she returned to the lobby, her hair swept up into a bun and dressed in a clean t-shirt with their motel's logo on it and her favorite pair of jean shorts – it was time to leave for lunch with Sam. She popped into the kennels to make sure none of the dogs needed anything, then grabbed her purse and hurried out the lobby door.

To her surprise, Sam's truck was already waiting in the parking lot. He always came in if he arrived before she was outside, but by the looks of it, he had been there long enough to shut the engine off and roll the driver's side window down. She saw him sitting in the driver's seat, his head turned as he watched someone else who was walking across the parking lot.

She walked over to the truck. Sam turned his head as she neared, his scruffy face softening into a warm smile when he saw her. She stooped to kiss him, then in a hushed voice said, "What's up? Why are you watching that guy?"

He took both hands off the steering wheel to sign back, *He's been walking around the parking lot for the past couple of minutes, checking the place out. Seemed weird, so I decided to keep an eye on him.*

She frowned and straightened up, taking a better look at the man who had caught Sam's attention. He was wearing a black ball cap pulled low over his face and mirrored sunglasses, a plain blueish-grey T-shirt, and jeans. He looked almost *too* unremarkable; someone she wouldn't have looked twice at normally, but now that Sam had pointed him out, she had to wonder if it was intentional.

Or maybe everything that was going on with Allison was making her paranoid.

"I don't think he's a guest," she said quietly. "I could be wrong, though. I'm going to go talk to him. I'll be right back."

She had no doubt that Sam would come to her rescue if something went wrong, but she doubted she had anything to be worried about.

She strode across the parking lot, and when she got close enough to the man, who was typing something on his phone, she called out, "Hi there, can I help you with something?"

The man looked up and slid his phone back into his pocket as he gave her a friendly smile. "Maybe. Do you work here?"

"I'm one of the owners," she said, coming to a stop a few feet away from him. "Sadie Barton. Do you have a room with us?"

He shook her hand. "Jake Derry. And no. Well, not yet. I'm doing dispersed camping in the state forest not far from here, and my first night was, ah… not very comfortable. I figured I'd scope out the local accommodations to see where the best place to go is if I decide I don't want to struggle through another night of mosquitos and weird noises. I usually avoid motels, but it seems like the only other option around here is a bed and breakfast that charges almost three times what you do."

Sadie relaxed immediately. It was clear he had done his research on where to stay in Greencreek, and she knew firsthand just how uncomfortable camping could be. There was always a lot more bugs and dirt than the movies showed.

"I might be biased, but I think we're pretty decent as far as motels go," she told him. Remembering the woman from yesterday who had complained that she couldn't get food delivered, she added, "As long as your expectations are reasonable, of course. Our rooms are clean, we have security cameras that actually work, and we even have some of the best cookies in the state for sale right here in our lobby. My business partner, Penny, is in there right now, if you'd like to talk to her about your concerns. I know motels don't have the best reputation, but I can promise our rooms are going to be a lot more comfortable than your tent."

"You know what, just talking to you has reassured me," he said. "You might see me again if I decide camping isn't for me."

She returned to Sam's truck, humming a little. Getting a new guest, or even just a potential one, was always a good feeling.

CHAPTER FIVE

They ate at The Creek Kitchen, but Sadie wasn't going to complain about eating a meal from the diner twice in as many days. The menu was varied enough that it was hard to get tired of what they offered, and it was a nice treat to eat in for once, instead of getting takeout.

Most of their conversation over lunch was focused on Allison and the problems she might have dragged with her to the motel. Sam was deeply worried, and kept putting his sandwich down to sign to her.

He thought they should back out of the contract with Allison immediately and ask her to get the trailer off their property by the end of the day. Sadie understood where he was coming from – he cared about her safety and well-being just like she cared about that of their dogs and guests – but it was hard to commit to taking that extreme measure when Allison herself wasn't even sure who had set the fire, let alone whether it was connected to her business. All she had to go on was the determination from the insurance fraud investigators that it was arson, and Sadie suspected their investigation might have been a little biased. Arson raised the possibility that Allison had set the fire herself, and that would mean they wouldn't have to pay out her claim.

"Look, I can't end the contract over something that might be nothing," Sadie said at last. "We're going to talk about it more this evening, but she said that if someone *is* behind this, they never outright tried to hurt her or anyone else. I can't make a decision until I learn more, and until Penny and I get a chance to discuss what we want to do. I know you're worried, Sam, but I'm going to be careful. I'm already planning to turn my notification volume to max tonight, and I'll set all of the cameras to alert me when they detect a person, even if it means I'll be woken up every couple hours by guests who get back late. I'm not going to take any chances."

I don't like this, he signed back, *but I can't tell you what to do. I'll keep my phone's volume turned up too. If something happens, if you even think you see someone suspicious, call and I'll be on my way over before the first ring ends.*

She knew he would make good on his promise, and it made her feel better to know that if something *did* happen, help would be just minutes away. Sam lived right next door to the motel in a house that had come along with the property parcel when they bought it. The residence and the motel were separated by a short path through the overgrown tree line. Sam could probably be at the motel before she had even finished putting her shoes on and getting down to the lobby, if he hurried.

She didn't want their whole date to be doom and gloom, so once Sam seemed to accept that nothing was going to change until they knew more about the situation, she changed the subject to something happier: the motel's upcoming one-year anniversary celebration. In just a few weeks it would be August, and she and Penny would have been in Greencreek for an entire twelve months. In that time, they had not only managed to get the rundown, abandoned motel and dog training and boarding business up and running, but they had managed to make the business somewhat profitable. It was a huge achievement, and she and Penny were planning on throwing a party to celebrate – a party that all of their guests, clients, and all the residents of Greencreek would be invited to – dogs included, of course.

The change of topic worked. By the time they finished their lunch and left the diner, Sam was smiling at her idea for an obstacle course that both kids and dogs could go through, complete with prizes for everyone who participated.

He paused by the truck to ask, *Do you want to get cookies on the way back?*

"Yeah, that sounds great," she said, grinning. "My treat since you got lunch."

Before he could object, she kissed him on the cheek and grabbed his hand, leading the way across the road and down the block to Sunshine Desserts.

The little cookie shop was usually packed full on weekends, but for some reason there was only one other customer inside when Sadie and Sam arrived. The reason for this became clear within seconds. The woman was fuming and shouting at Bailey, who looked like she was at the end of her rope.

"Are you kidding me? I'm trying to warn people about someone who is a risk to their dogs! Don't you care about animals? Do you want to see someone else lose their beloved pet?"

"Miss, I already said I'm not going to let you put that flyer up in Sunshine Desserts, and my answer is not going to change. This is the third time I'm asking you to leave. If I have to ask you again, I will call the police."

The woman let out a frustrated sound like a quiet scream, crumpled the paper she was holding, threw it directly at Bailey's face – the other woman managed to dodge so the balled up paper flew over her shoulder instead – and spun on her heel to stomp toward the door. She came to a sudden stop when she saw Sadie and Sam. Her eyes flicked from Sadie's face down to her shirt, then back up to her face again.

"Shoot," Bailey muttered from behind the counter.

"I'm Deborah Franklin," the woman said, striding over to them and shoving her hand at Sadie aggressively. She was wearing a pantsuit and had a short, elegant haircut. "You work at that motel on Highway 78, correct?"

Sadie gave her hand a brief shake, more out of reflex than anything, and said, "I'm one of the owners, yes." She glanced past the woman's shoulder at Bailey, who was shaking her head and mouthing something at her.

"So, you're the person responsible for hiring Allison Mason, I take it? I can only assume you weren't aware of her full history when you hired her."

It had recently become clear to Sadie that she didn't know anywhere near enough about Allison's past, and that made the woman's words sting all the more for being true. "I did look into her history, but didn't see any major red flags when I hired her. If you have a particular concern, I would like to hear it. The safety of the dogs is my number one priority."

"I used to be a client of Allison's until she stole my dog," Deborah said, "and I'm not the only one she did that to, either. I know at least four other people who lost their dogs because of her, and I wouldn't be surprised if that number is even higher, and some of her victims just aren't talking.

"She stole your dog?" Sadie said. She didn't know what she was expecting, but it wasn't that. "I'm not saying I don't believe you, but do you have proof?"

In response, Deborah turned to Bailey and snapped her fingers. "Give me back that flyer." She turned back to Sadie and explained, "My phone number, contact information, and the online group I made for people who have been hurt or lost their dogs because of Allison is all right there. And shame on you for hiring this woman without doing proper research first."

With that, she brushed past Sadie and Sam and

pushed her way through the door. Bailey had already stooped to pick up the crumpled piece of paper.

"You two came in at the worst possible time," she said. "You'll see when you look at the flyer, but she's trying to get people to boycott your motel until you fire Allison. I told her that there was no way I was letting her put the flyer up in here — not only do I have a partnership with Sit, Stay, Sleep, so I'd be shooting myself in the foot, but I also consider you and Penny friends. I think that woman's out of her mind."

"I hope you're right," Sadie said as she took the crumpled ball of paper and smoothed it out, "but I'm still going to look into it."

She and Sam got their cookies, but her mood was ruined. She stared at the crumpled flyer all the way home. There was a photo of a small dog, a Shih Tzu, front and center, then the contact information, a brief explanation of why *exactly* Deborah thought the motel should be boycotted, and some bold testimonials from other people who had had similar experiences with Allison. Sadie still didn't quite understand what was going on. How could Allison have stolen multiple clients' dogs? She was pretty sure the police would get involved if something like that was happening.

When they returned to the motel, Sam parked and they both undid their seatbelts. They were planning to eat the cookies inside with Jasper and Penny, and then maybe go on a short walk through the woods with Jasper, Briar, and Rose, Sam's two redbone coonhounds, if they had time.

No sooner had Sadie stepped out of the truck than she heard a "Yoo-hoo!" from the north side of the motel, where Allison's grooming trailer was, and saw a woman round the corner and make a beeline across the parking lot toward her. For a second, Sadie saw the woman's brown hair and thought she was Allison, but her voice and stride were all wrong. A second later, she realized she was the woman who had been chewing Penny out for not hand delivering her food all the way from Burns. What was her name? She thought Penny had addressed her as Barbara.

She let out a quiet groan as the woman approached them. Sam shot her a curious look, but Sadie didn't have time to explain. Barbara, or whatever her name was, was already halfway across the parking lot, her lips pressed together so tightly that they had almost vanished. Sadie was struggling to paste a professional customer service smile on her face when a deafening crack split the air and the woman in front of her collapsed to the ground.

CHAPTER SIX

At first, Sadie was too confused to react. It took her brain a few seconds to link the noise with the woman's collapse. When she did, she realized the sound she heard must have been a gunshot. One of their guests had just been shot right in front of her.

Her body jerked into motion, but before she made it more than a few steps, an arm slid around her waist and pulled her back against a solid chest. Sam. He pulled her with him into a crouch behind his truck.

Stay here, he signed. *The shooter is still out there.*

He leaned around the side of the truck to scan the woods across the road. Sadie felt like everything was moving in slow motion. She was torn between sickening worry for the woman who was laying motionless on the asphalt and a sharper, gut-deep fear for

Sam, whose head and shoulders were exposed as he looked for whoever had shot Barbara.

Suddenly, Sam burst into motion, taking off running from behind the truck. Sadie yelled out after him, "What are you doing? You're going to get shot!" but he kept going, vanishing into the woods.

She stared after him, then glanced back at Barbara. She had never felt so torn in her life. In the end, she wrenched herself away from the dark forest where Sam had vanished, presumably chasing the person who shot Barbara, and moved towards the woman instead. She didn't think she would be able to catch up to Sam, and she wasn't sure it would help if she did. She was afraid she would just be a distraction.

And Barbara was right there, injured and possibly dying just feet away from her. She might not like the woman very much but she was still a human being, and a guest… and she needed help.

Her heart racing and her ears primed for another gunshot – if she heard one, she was going after Sam no matter what – she hurried across the distance between Sam's truck and where Barbara lay in the middle of the parking lot. The back of her neck prickled, but she knew the shooter wouldn't have time to let off another shot at the motel if Sam was chasing after him.

The trees across the road remained silent, and Sadie reached Barbara safely. She dropped to her knees, ignoring the scrape of the asphalt on her knees, and turned the woman over. At first, she thought the fact that there wasn't much blood was a good sign, but Barbara's stillness told her something was wrong. Sadie checked for a pulse or any sign that the woman was breathing but failed to find either.

The bullet had struck her right over her heart. Sadie was the furthest thing from a medical expert, but she suspected the woman had died instantly.

The lobby door opened and Penny rushed outside, her eyes wild as she raced over to where Sadie was kneeling next to Barbara. She realized it had been less than a minute since the gun went off, even though the time seemed to have stretched out much longer than that.

"What happened?" her friend asked, clutching her phone as she stared down at them. "I heard a noise – was that a gun going off?"

"Someone shot her," Sadie said. Her hands were shaking, but her voice was matter of fact. "Call 911. Sam went after the shooter."

Penny dialed the number and pressed the phone to

her ear, the fingers of her other hand pressed to her lips until the dispatcher answered. Sadie couldn't focus on the conversation… she rose to her feet and turned to look across the road, where the forest seemed to have eaten Sam. The little bag of cookies lay forgotten on the ground next to the truck.

"Sadie. *Sadie.*" When she saw that she finally had her attention, Penny said, "The first responders are on their way. Are you hurt? Is Sam?"

Sadie shook her head. "I'm fine. But he's out there–"

She broke off when she spotted movement in the trees. She took a step backward reflexively, her muscled coiled as she waited for another gunshot to split the air, only to nearly collapse with release when she realized it was Sam. He stepped out of the trees, and she hurried to meet him halfway across the road. It was sheer luck that no one was speeding down the highway, because she didn't stop to check.

She threw herself into his arms, and felt his arms tighten around her. "I was so worried about you," she babbled into his shoulder. "She's dead, the guest. Barbara."

His hand smoothed down her back, then he withdrew from the hug but took her hand and urged her across the street to the relative shelter of the parking lot. She spotted a few of their other guests gathering on the sidewalk in front of the rooms. Some distant part of her mind warned that this was going to be bad for the motel. Very bad.

Police? Sam signed as soon as they reached Penny, who was crouched beside Barbara, listening intently to whatever the dispatcher was saying over the phone.

"They're on their way," Sadie told him. "Did you see who it was?"

He shook his head. *I think they ran as soon as they got the shot off. I heard someone moving away from me, but I couldn't catch them.*

"That's probably good," she said. "They had a *gun*, Sam. You weren't even armed. Not even with that ax you tried to chase us away with the first time we met."

Normally the memory of their first meeting made both of them chuckle, but there was no levity in the mention of it then. *I'd rather they were focused on me than on you, or Penny, or the motel,* he signed. When she frowned, he added, *It's harder to hit a moving target, anyway.*

She didn't want to argue with him, not right now. Instead, she just stepped into his arms again and let him hold her. "I'm just glad you're okay," she said. "I don't know what I'd do if I lost you."

Normally, the admission might have made her feel too vulnerable – they hadn't even said "I love you" yet, and she didn't want to seem like she was too clingy – but right now she was just too shocked and horrified to care. Sam's arms tightened around her in response, since he couldn't use sign language while he was hugging her. It was one of the few times she found herself wishing he could talk.

They only broke apart when they heard the sirens. It hadn't been very long, but it still felt like an eternity to Sadie. Their other guests were huddled near their rooms, and a couple of them were filming. As the sirens got louder, Allison walked around the building from the spot where her grooming trailer was parked. Her face was flushed, and she had a leaf and a couple of twigs in her hair. Sadie's focus immediately narrowed to Allison and only Allison, and she left the comfort of Sam's nearness to stride across the parking lot toward her.

"Where were you?" she asked, her voice sharper than she intended.

Allison stopped short, taken aback. "I was taking a walk along the paths behind the motel. Georgia cancelled her appointment at the last minute, so I decided to get some exercise. What happened out here? I hurried back as soon as I heard the sirens."

"One of our guests was shot," Sadie said, not sure whether she should believe Allison or not. "Didn't you hear the gun go off?"

"Well, sure, but I couldn't tell where it came from. I just figured someone was hunting nearby." She looked past Sadie, to where Barbara still lay on the asphalt, and her face paled. "Someone really got shot? Is she okay?"

"No," Sadie said shortly.

Before she could elaborate, the sound of the sirens grew almost deafening, then suddenly fell silent as an ambulance that looked like it was older than she was pulled into the parking lot. The local sheriff's patrol vehicle was right behind it.

Sadie returned to her place near Sam and Penny as the paramedics jumped out of the ambulance and began to check Barbara over. The sheriff was a little slower to follow, and when he did, he observed the paramedics and briefly spoke to one of them before he walked over to where they were waiting, out of the way.

"None of you are hurt?" His gaze lingered on Penny, who shook her head. "Good. Start talking."

CHAPTER SEVEN

Both of the sheriff's deputies arrived while Sadie and Sam were still answering Sheriff Islington's questions. They began to comb the woods for evidence, but when they left hours later, they had come up empty-handed. Sheriff Islington looked unhappy, but Sadie doubted he blamed his hard-working deputies for their lack of success. The Greencreek sheriff's department didn't get much in the way of funding, and Sadie knew their resources were limited. This was the sort of investigation that the state police would probably have to take over. While they had access to and funding for high-tech labs, those same labs were often backed up for weeks.

Unless the killer made a mistake, their arrest would be anything but quick... which meant they were still out there somewhere, and still a threat to everyone in town.

"I wish we had dogs," he muttered as he scanned the tree line one last time. "We could really use the noses on those coonhounds of yours, Sam."

Sam nodded and signed, *We're going to start training them soon, but they need a handler.*

Sadie knew he was upset that he wouldn't be able to be his own dogs' handler when they started their search and rescue and tracking careers, but the fact that he couldn't talk meant he couldn't use a radio to communicate, and couldn't call out if he found someone. The limitations ate at him, but there was no magic solution. He would be a part of the dogs' training, but he knew he wouldn't be the one out there with them while they were working.

Sheriff Islington looked to Sadie for translation, so she obliged, then added, "I'm planning on starting in September. I need to do a little research first. I know the theory behind training working scent detection dogs, but I've never actually done it before. I know someone who's involved with search and rescue up in Michigan and trains her own dogs, so I'm going to reach out to her and see if she's willing to share some tips and advice."

The sheriff nodded and left them with a warning

to be careful, because the shooter was still out there and they didn't know what he or she wanted yet, or if they were going to strike again, and a demand that they close the motel for the rest of the weekend. Sadie already knew they were going to lose a lot of business over this, but she couldn't bring herself to care. It would be for the best if their guests left, since she didn't want anyone else to be in danger.

Penny began knocking on doors to give updates to the guests who were here, and Sadie went inside to call all of the guests who were currently out and about, enjoying what should have been a perfect – if rather sweltering – summer Saturday. She also emailed everyone who had made a reservation for the coming week to let them know their reservations would likely be cancelled and they should start looking for other plans. The sheriff might be okay with them reopening after the weekend if nothing else happened, but she wasn't sure she and Penny would be ready.

When she finished, she went into the back to check on Jasper and the boarding dogs. None of them seemed worried, though she was sure the sirens must have stressed them out a little. She closed all of the sliding doors between the indoor kennels and the outdoor runs just in case the shooter came back now that the police presence was gone. The runs were visible from the woods behind the motel, and she wasn't going to take any chances. Installing a fence suddenly felt like a much higher priority than it had been. Preferably a tall, wooden privacy fence that blocked view of the dogs from all angles.

Sam stuck close by her side while she did all of this. When they returned to the lobby, Penny was busy at the front desk, checking out and refunding their guests. Good… they would be safer somewhere else.

"When you go home, you should go out the back and walk through the trees to your property," she said in a low voice to Sam. "If someone's watching the parking lot, they won't be able to see you. You can come back after dark to get your truck."

I'm not leaving anytime soon, he signed back to her.

"What about your dogs?"

I let them outside just before I left for lunch. They're in the house, and the doors are locked. I installed a camera inside so I can check on them while I'm working. They'll be fine. Bored, but safe. I need to make sure you stay safe, too.

"You should go get them," she said. "Deputy Francis is acting as a deterrent right now. Bring them over, and we can put them in the kennels until the lobby clears out. That way they'll be here, and you won't have to worry about going to get them later. You could... you could spend the night, if you want."

He hesitated, as if he didn't want to leave her for even a second, but finally gave a brief nod, pressed a kiss to her temple, and hurried outside. He returned before Penny had finished refunding their guests, the two big red dogs by his side and a duffel bag slung over his shoulder. As she watched them walk past the crowd of strangers, she felt a tiny surge of satisfaction at the reminder of how much their behavior had improved. When he first adopted them, the two dogs had been used to living without any boundaries or rules. They were both good natured, but they were large, rambunctious, and rude, especially Briar. Now, they walked calmly past the long line of guests with Sam without pulling or trying to jump up on anyone.

Still, they were big dogs, and she knew they had at least one guest with pet allergies – they only had one allergy friendly room, and she knew Penny had checked someone into it a couple days ago – so she brought Sam into the back so he could put the dogs in their two free kennels. She filled up clean water bowls for them, gave them each one of the extra dog beds they kept in the storage room, and passed them each one of Jasper's bully sticks to keep them occupied. That led to her passing out treats to all of the dogs. Since they couldn't go outside, they were sure to be bored.

By the time they returned to the lobby, Penny was almost through with the line of guests and Allison had joined them. She had brushed her hair and her face was pale rather than flushed as she sat primly in one of the uncomfortable waiting chairs on the other side of the room. Sadie ignored her for now and walked over to the front desk instead to see if she could make Penny's job any easier.

Only when the last guest left did they turn their attention to Allison, who was wringing her hands together.

"I should go before the deputy leaves," she said quietly. "But I wanted to talk to you first. I… I think this is my fault."

"Explain," Sadie said, crossing her arms. The thought had already crossed her mind. Allison had warned them someone might be after her, and then something like this happens? She couldn't ignore the coincidence.

Allison looked devastated as she spoke. "The woman who died, she was talking to me right before it happened. She had come from the lobby looking for another employee. I guess Penny was on the phone or something."

Penny nodded. "I remember that. Someone put me on hold while they checked their schedule to see which nights they needed to make a reservation for. I asked Barbara to come back later, mostly because I just didn't want to deal with whatever new complaint she had just then."

"Well, she found me next. I told her I didn't work for the motel and didn't have anything to do with that side of things, but either she didn't believe me or she didn't care because she started complaining about how the water was too hard and it was wrecking her hair, and she wanted the motel to pay for the trip to the stylist she would have to take when she went home. Honestly, I tuned her out for most of it. Anyway, at some point she compared our hair and mentioned how similar we look. Then, just a few seconds after she left *my trailer* someone shot her. They must have thought they were aiming at me. It's the only thing that makes sense, especially when combined with the arson and the other weird things that have been happening to me."

"Hold on," Sadie said. "I thought you were taking a walk when the gun went off."

"Well, it was more of a jog," Allison said. "I left

as soon as she did. I was frustrated and wanted to get some energy out. I was already behind the motel when I heard the gunshot and couldn't tell how close it was. I only started coming back when I heard the sirens."

Something about the explanation didn't sit right with her, but Allison held her gaze earnestly. Finally, Penny broke the silence.

"You need to tell Sheriff Islington everything, Allison, and I think it would be best for everyone if you let your clients know you're not going to be able to see them for a while. I think I speak for all of us when I say we want you and everyone else to stay safe, and right now the motel is probably the least safe place you could be."

Allison nodded, the motion tight and jerky. "Yeah. I figured. I'll cancel this week's appointments as soon as I get home. And I understand if you want to back out of the contract. I won't try to fight it or hold it against you. But… I hope you know I *never* thought anything like this would happen. I wasn't even certain someone was trying to hurt me. I wanted to believe I was just being paranoid. I would never put anyone in danger knowingly."

"I don't think any of us expected something like this to happen," Sadie said. "For now, just go home, try to recover, and be safe. I'm sure Deputy Francis would escort you back to your house if you asked. I have a lot more questions for you, but they can wait until later. I don't think any of us are in a good place for that sort of discussion right now. We all need some time to process, and to figure out where to go from here."

CHAPTER EIGHT

Even after Allison left, none of them did much other than sit there. Sadie made sure the lobby door was locked and drew the curtains while Penny, who had briefly gone back to Room Three to get her overnight essentials, went upstairs to Sadie's apartment to talk to her parents privately and make sure all of the windows up there were locked. Sam made sure the back door in the kennel room was locked, then brought Briar, Rose, and Jasper back to the lobby with him. Sadie, who was sitting behind the front desk talking to Cody, who had taken Angus home with him for the weekend again, patted her thighs to encourage Jasper to jump up, and buried her face in the foxhound's soft neck. His simple joy at seeing her eased something in her heart. Jasper lived in a world where, as long as they were together, everything was all right, and being around him helped her narrow her mind to the present moment rather than dwelling on the past or the what-ifs of the future.

It wasn't until the lobby phone rang and she answered it to find her very confused client on the other end that she remembered her afternoon private dog training lesson, which she had completely missed. Thankfully, the owners of the nervous little Chihuahua she had been working with were understanding when she told them an emergency had come up and she would have to reschedule.

None of them left the main part of the motel again that evening. Even the dogs only got to go out briefly in their runs after dark, and she made sure all the kennels were closed up tight after that. She had already notified the owners of the boarding dogs about the incident, but many of them were hours or even states away and couldn't get back quickly to pick up their dogs. A couple of them had emergency contacts who could pick their dogs up tomorrow, but Sadie was the one responsible for their well-being until then.

Sam stayed in the lobby on the cot he kept in their laundry room that night, their protector, while Penny slept in Sadie's apartment, on her couch. Sadie slept fitfully in her own bed, and Jasper, who usually slept by her feet or sprawled across her legs, must have been able to tell how upset she was because he slept cuddled up against her back, his warm chin resting in the crook of her neck.

Sunday passed achingly slowly, but uneventfully. The sheriff kept one of his deputies posted out front for most of the day and promised he would arrange for regular law enforcement presence at the motel for the coming week. There were no more gunshots, no more bodies falling to the ground, but Sadie and her friends were still reluctant to so much as peek outside.

By Monday, things began to get back to normal, if only by necessity. Sam had to go to work, though he left Rose and Briar at the kennel since the dogs would be more entertained at the motel and they only had two boarding dogs left so Sadie's load was light. She and Penny decided to hold off on making a decision about when to reopen the motel rooms for another couple of days, at least, and Allison agreed to come over on Tuesday to tell them everything that had happened to her in the months before she lost her trailer to arson. Sadie also wanted to ask her about everything Deborah Franklin had said. If anything, that line of questioning was even more important now, since if Allison's theory about who the killer had *really* been aiming for was right… then she might have been the intended victim. Finding out who exactly had a grudge against her might be the quickest way to solve the case and feel safe at their own motel again.

Alone, Penny and Sadie sat in the lobby to discuss their next steps, and decided to invest in another security camera that they could aim directly across the road, rather than at the parking lot and lobby entrance, or down the row of rooms like their current cameras did. A call to the local hardware store confirmed that Norma had the updated version of the security cameras they had bought last year in stock. It was a little more expensive, but was supposed to have advanced night vision that would hopefully let them see into the dark trees a little better. It wasn't a solution, not really, but it would make them both feel a little better to know that they would be able to check the tree line from a distance. She didn't think either of them would get over having a guest shot dead in their parking lot any time soon, which meant they were going to be jumpy and paranoid for a long time to come.

One of them would need to drive into town to get the camera, and Sadie was the one who volunteered for the task. She would take the fleeting stress of being exposed while she walked out to her SUV over being stuck at the motel alone, letting her thoughts consume her.

Once she was safely on the road, she realized how good it felt to leave the dreary motel after being cooped up for so long. She wasn't in a hurry to get back, so she spent a while chatting with Norma after she paid for the camera. Mulberry, the elderly beagle Norma had adopted a few months ago, waddled over to her and flopped over on her side so Sadie could scratch her belly, and Norma listened quietly while she told her what happened. The news had already spread around town, but things always got twisted in the game of telephone that was gossip, and she wanted her friends to know the truth.

After leaving the hardware store, she put the camera in her SUV, then looked across the street at the diner, wondering if she should pick up something to take back to the motel. They had been living off of the frozen meals she had in her freezer, which wasn't helping the general feeling of depression at the motel. Maybe she should just go to the grocery store and get some ingredients to make something fresh–

"Sadie!"

She turned at the sound of her name to see Bailey standing in Sunshine Desserts' doorway, waving at her. Putting her food plans on hold, Sadie walked the short distance down the block toward her.

"I'm glad I spotted you," Bailey said as she drew closer. "Garrick was just saying he wanted to talk to you."

"Garrick?"

Bailey glanced over her shoulder, then shielded the side of her mouth and whispered, "You know, that homeless guy. He said he knows you."

Sadie glanced through the window and saw Garrick Washington standing near the counter, his long grey hair drawn back into a tangled ponytail and a fraying backpack on his back.

"I know who he is," Sadie whispered back. "I was just surprised *you* knew him."

"Oh, I must have forgotten to tell you. Remember when someone set the cookie shop on fire a couple weeks ago and I said I was going to look into getting security?" She turned to gesture at Garrick, who was watching them so she ended up turning the gesture into a smile and wave. "Well, he's my security. He's been checking in on the place at night, and he said if I ever have problems with someone in the future, he's happy to hang out during the day too and make sure no one causes trouble. I'm paying him, of course, but I've also been slipping him free food when I can.

He's actually pretty nice once you start talking to him."

"He saved my life a while ago," Sadie said. "I've been helping him out when I can, too. I'm happy to see what he wants."

She followed Bailey inside, inhaling the sweet, buttery vanilla scent that seemed to be permanently embedded in the walls. Garrick nodded at her in greeting.

"Good to see you're all right. I heard you had a spot of trouble at that motel of yours."

"More than just a spot," Sadie said. "I guess I should be grateful only one person got hurt."

He grunted in response. "Well, if you want an extra set of eyes to make sure nothing like that happens again, I'm happy to camp out somewhere nearby, but that's not what I wanted to talk to you about. I figure you must have a lot of empty rooms right now. I met this guy who's been trying to make a go of camping out not far from one of my spots, but he's been struggling and a storm's supposed to roll in tonight. Thought maybe I'd try to talk him in to heading your way, before he drowns in his tent. These woods aren't any place for a city boy during a storm."

Something about that sounded familiar. "Is his name Jake?"

Garrick nodded, surprised. "You know him?"

"He already stopped by the motel to see if he'd want to stay there if camping got to be too much for him." She hesitated. "We haven't officially re-opened yet, but unless he wants to stay at the bed and breakfast, there aren't exactly many other places he could go. I'd rather offer him a room than know he's out there, caught in a storm he isn't prepared for. Just make sure to tell him *why* we're closed, all right? He needs to know the risks. And if you need a place to stay, Garrick–"

"I appreciate it, but I love being out in these summer storms. I've got my hidey-holes, don't worry about me. But I'll pass the message along. Seen these woods make too many people disappear. Just like a dog, they'll bite ya if you don't show them respect."

CHAPTER NINE

Sadie returned to the motel bearing lunch and cookies, just enough for her and Penny, plus an almond cookie for whenever Sam dropped by, since they had told Cody he didn't need to come in today.

With no guests and only two boarding dogs, it was the quietest day Sadie had experienced in a long time. If it wasn't for the heavy weight of her guilt and grief over Barbara's death, the fact that their parking lot seemed to have turned into the local law enforcement's favorite break spot – something she was grateful for, even if it was a constant reminder of what happened, and the looming decision to be made about Allison, plus worry for the other woman's well-being, Sadie would have enjoyed the time off.

As it was, with the woods off limits and only so

much cleaning that could be done, they were almost forced to spend their time taking care of business on the computer. Jasper and the two coonhounds lazed on the cool tile floor while Sadie and Penny sat squished together in front of the laptop, finalizing their plans for the party in August. They were being optimistic, hoping that this latest tragedy would be nothing but a dark memory by then. Refreshments, food – preferably from local businesses – entertainment for adults, kids, and dogs all alike, gift bags of prizes they could give away, fun contests anyone could enjoy… Sadie realized it was practically turning into a small festival, and wondered if they were being *too* optimistic.

They got some more productive tasks done, too, including scheduling a consultation with an IT company to see how difficult it would be to get an intercom system installed with their cinder block walls.

The sun crossed the sky outside as their productivity dwindled. It was a hot day, even with the air conditioning going full blast. Sadie was tempted to take a cue from the dogs and lay flat on the cool tiles. It was too hot to venture upstairs for a nap. Her cheap window AC unit couldn't compete with the heat and humidity of a day like today.

All of the dogs got homemade popsicles made out of low sodium chicken broth, and she and Penny split the rest of her ice cream, making cookie sandwiches out of some of the cookies from their display case – cookies which were on their way to stale. Sadie had cancelled their usual Tuesday order of cookies while she was at Sunshine Desserts: no guests meant no one to buy them.

She had almost forgotten that Garrick had said he was going to try to convince Jake Derry, inexperienced city boy, to go to the motel that night. It was the slow rumble of thunder as evening fell that reminded her. She stepped outside through the back of the kennel while the dogs sniffed around their outdoor runs for the first time that night and looked at the sky. The sun was already low, behind the trees, but a storm cloud rose like dark mountains to the south.

A dark and stormy night. Hopefully, it would cool things off a little. The lobby had begun to feel smothering, and neither of them felt safe enough to leave the door propped open, even with the heat.

Penny felt brave enough to move back into her room that night, and retired early, likely to watch a movie, drink some wine, and try to escape from their depressing reality before bed. Sam had shown up earlier to get Rose and Briar. He had offered to stay again, but she told him to go home and get some rest. She felt better having Sam here, but she was an adult woman. She didn't need someone to stand guard while she slept.

She was too restless from doing nothing all day to attempt to go to bed early, and she was still half expecting Jake to show up, probably bedraggled and muddy from being caught out in the rain, so she stayed in the lobby, watching videos on her phone about how to build a DIY agility course while Jasper chewed on a toy in the middle of the floor.

She was unsurprised, even a bit relieved, when she heard a car turn into the parking lot from the road and saw the cut of headlights through the deluge. She got up, peered out the window, and unlocked the lobby door as someone rushed inside. Sure enough, it was Jake Derry, and he looked even more bedraggled and pitiful than she had expected.

"Man, that guy wasn't joking about the storms out here," he muttered, shaking himself off like a dog on the durable rug just inside the door. "Please tell me you have vacancies. That old guy said you had rooms open, but when I looked online it said you weren't accepting reservations—"

"We have available rooms," Sadie said, ushering him in further and shutting the door behind him. "Did

Garrick tell you *why* we're not accepting reservations right now?"

"Something about a shooting in the parking lot?" he asked, wiping rainwater that dripped down his forehead and into his eyes. "I don't care about that. I just need somewhere dry to sleep."

"Then let's get you checked in," she said. "Just one night?"

"Might as well make it two," he said with a grimace. "I left some of my stuff out there, and I doubt I'll want to drive home after spending half a day hiking through the muddy woods to get back to my camping spot."

She marked it down on the schedule. "Your checkout time will be at eleven Wednesday morning."

She checked his driver's license, recorded the ID number, accepted his payment — a couple of soaking wet bills — and waved Jasper away from where he was sniffing the man's boots.

"I'll put you in Room Nine," she said. "It's the second to last down the row, but it's furthest from the kennels, which means the dogs shouldn't bother you if they bark during the night." He looked like he could use the rest.

"Thank you," he said. "You're a lifesaver."

She locked the lobby door behind him when he

left, and watched through the window as he fetched a long duffel bag from the back of his sporty SUV. Then she took her phone out to check the cameras until she saw that he had made it safely into Room Nine. With their only guest snug in his room for the night, she decided to go upstairs after all. Maybe Penny had the right idea and it was time to find an escape from the world, no matter how briefly it lasted.

She was halfway through her kennel chores the next morning when she heard honking coming from the parking lot. She expected Penny to deal with whatever was going on — the last time she saw her friend, she was in the lobby on the phone with Sheriff Islington, trying to determine whether it was safe to officially reopen the motel to the public. When the honking continued, Sadie put down her mop with a grumble and hurried out front in her damp scrubs. Last night's storm had brought the temperature down a few degrees, but it was chokingly humid.

The group of five who were currently blocking the motel's entrance with their pickets and signs didn't seem intimidated by the humidity in the slightest. Jake was the one who was honking, since they were blocking his way out of the parking lot. Penny was standing on the grass near the curb and ineffectively trying to get their attention as they chanted, "*Boycott bad groomers!*"

"What is going on?" Sadie shouted as she jogged over.

Her and Penny's combined presence finally drew the attention of one of the protesters — Deborah. She recognized the woman from their confrontation at Sunshine Desserts. Deborah looked angry but also more than a little exhilarated as the other continued chanting.

"We're protesting Allison Mason," she said, "and we're prepared to be out here every single day until we chase her out of the area."

CHAPTER TEN

Sadie didn't know what to make of an honest to goodness protest, against a dog groomer of all people, and Penny looked just as clueless as she was. The commotion must have reached Sam's house, because he walked over from his property and stood shoulder to shoulder with Sadie, staring at the small group that was walking back and forth across the parking lot's entrance.

Jake didn't let off the horn the entire time. Sadie knocked on his window to talk to him, and he briefly let the obnoxious sound stop for a second to tell her, "If they're going to be annoying, so am I. I'm not going to stop until they move."

For the sake of her own burgeoning headache, Sadie was close to begging him to lay off the horn but decided to leave him to it. They didn't have any other guests, after all, and as much as she supported the very American right to protest, she wasn't exactly thrilled about it happening right in front of her motel.

In the end, after a hurried internet search that uncovered some confusing laws, Penny ended up calling Sheriff Islington, who drove down to the motel to talk to the protesters. He seemed far too amused by the whole thing. Sadie suspected he was grateful to get a call from the motel that wasn't deadly serious.

After making it clear to the protestors they couldn't go onto the motel's private property and couldn't block the road, he left them to it. They grudgingly parted so Jake could drive through, then returned to their march.

"Sorry, y'all," he said as he approached Penny and Sadie where they were standing in the shade of the motel. "There isn't much I can do as long as they aren't causing an obstruction to traffic or trespassing. The road's public property, and so is all the land surrounding the parcel the motel is on."

"At least they picked a good day to do it," Penny muttered. "It's not like they're going to drive anyone away."

"Shoot," Sadie muttered. "Allison." She shared a

wide-eyed look with Penny, then hurried inside to call the other woman and let her know about the situation. If she arrived while the protestors were there, it was sure to be a disaster.

She ended the call with a promise to tell Allison when the protestors left, and then, resigning herself to the sound of Deborah and the others protesting outside, she got back to work. As annoying as the constant noise was, she ended up bringing the rest of the cookies from their display case out around lunchtime — they were going to go stale otherwise, and she never liked wasting food.

The gesture seemed to take some of the wind out of Deborah's sails.

"You know, it's nothing personal against the motel," she said as she selected a lemon-frosted sugar cookie, "but Allison wronged us, and we have to stand up for what we believe in."

Whatever the group's issue with Allison was, it was important enough to keep them going throughout most of the day, though the chanting and marching began to lose some steam as the hottest part of the day came and went. She and Penny had taken to watching them through the lobby window, half afraid they were going to get heat stroke, but finally, just as the sun was beginning to dip behind the trees, they packed up and left.

"Want to bet on whether they'll be back tomorrow?" Penny muttered from next to Sadie.

"Please, no," Sadie murmured. She had her Level One Obedience class tomorrow, and while she was thinking of moving it to a local park anyway, just to be on the safe side, the presence of the protestors all but made her decision for her.

Only time would tell whether they would be back, but at least they were gone for now. She waved through the window as Jake pulled into the parking lot – she had seen him drive past twice while the protestors were still there, apparently deciding it wasn't worth the trouble of trying to get through them again – then let herself flop into the spinning chair behind the front desk.

She snatched up her cell phone to call Allison. They needed to talk to her, needed to get the full story, not just of why Deborah was protesting in the first place, but also what other hints there had been that made Allison believe someone was out for her blood.

Allison sounded resigned when Sadie called, but she agreed to be there in forty-five minutes. As tempted as Sadie was to invite Sam over so he could hear Allison's story firsthand, it wouldn't be very professional for her boyfriend to be involved in an important talk with one of their staff. She would just have to catch him up later.

It was almost completely dark out by the time Allison arrived. She parked as close to the door as possible and hurried inside, reaching over to tug the curtains across the window before she turned back to them.

"Sorry, I'm still jumpy," she said. "You haven't had any other trouble here, have you?"

"Other than the protest earlier, no," Sadie said.

Allison grimaced. "Right, that."

"I think that's a good place to start," Penny said, hopping up to sit on the edge of the front desk. "What is this Sadie told me about stolen dogs? I know there must be *something* going on — no one is going to march back and forth, chanting, in this kind of humidity unless they have a good reason."

Allison sank into one of the uncomfortable chairs across from where Sadie and Penny were at the front desk, making the whole thing feel even more like an interrogation. Jasper, who had gotten up from his place on his dog bed to greet her, seemed to sense nothing fun was going to happen and flopped down on the floor with a dramatic groan. Allison glanced at him, then fixed her attention on Penny and Sadie with a sigh.

"Did Deborah really say I stole her dog?" she muttered. "I can't believe she's twisting things so much."

"Well, what's the truth?" Sadie asked, hopping up onto the desk next to Penny, her feet dangling a few inches above the floor. "Missing and stolen dogs are a serious accusation, especially for someone who works with animals professionally."

"The dogs aren't *stolen*," Allison said. She crossed her arms defiantly. "They were removed by animal control."

Sadie blinked. She hadn't been expecting that.

"All five of them?" she asked. She knew neglect and abuse happened, but thankfully she hadn't run across it too much in her own career.

"Yes, but it was over the past ten years," Allison said. "Deborah is the one who somehow tracked all of the others down and made them into her own little twisted cult of followers. She had this adorable little Shih Tzu, Ana, but she never brought her in often enough. Whenever she *did,* the dog's nails were horribly overgrown, almost growing into her paw pads. Her coat was matted and dirty, and she seemed to weigh less each time I saw her. Normally, if a dog comes in in bad condition, we clean it up as best we can and offer the owner assistance and advice, as long as it doesn't need a vet. The fact that they brought it in means they're trying, and we want to help people who want to be better, but this was consistent neglect over nearly a year of her being my client, and the last time she brought the dog in, she had a serious skin infection from the mats and she was practically skin and bone. I called animal control, and they took the dog away with them and pressed charges on Deborah. I saw Ana a couple months later in her foster home, and she was like a completely different dog. I definitely made the right choice. The others were all similar situations, where I felt like I had to step in for the welfare of the dog because whatever the issue was wasn't getting better. I never heard from any of the others again, but Deborah would *not* stop harassing me after the fact. I even had a restraining order on her, but she turned to harassing me online, making fake accounts to flood my web page with bad reviews, and just in general being a huge nuisance."

Allison's story sounded plausible, a lot more so than a groomer somehow getting away with stealing her clients' dogs over the years.

"Can you send us any information about the cases?" she asked, just to be on the safe side.

Allison nodded. "I have pictures of the conditions the dogs were in, and I have emails from animal control going back years. I document everything very carefully, but it hasn't stopped her from driving away quite a few clients over the years."

"Do you think she's the one behind the fire?" Penny asked. "And... the shooting?"

Allison's lips pursed. "I thought about it, of course, and I told Sheriff Islington about her. But why would she escalate now, after almost two years? She's been an annoyance, but as far as I know, she's never done anything criminal. Not to me, anyway."

"What else happened?" Sadie asked. At Allison's confused look, she added, "You mentioned there were other suspicious events before the fire."

"Oh, right. This was a few weeks before the fire, but I had someone spray-paint nasty words on the side of the truck that I used to pull my trailer around. I had to pay a lot to get the paint professionally removed. A few times, an unknown number called me, and when I answered, it was just breathing on the other end. And more than once, I caught someone lurking around my house late at night. Once, peeping in a window, and the other time standing in the bushes by the sidewalk in front of my house, just... staring."

"Did you call the police?" Penny asked.

"I didn't," Allison admitted. "Not until the fire, anyway. I didn't think they would take me seriously."

"It sounds like you've had this stalker for a while," Sadie said.

She was more worried about Allison than mad at her, now. Sure, the other woman had ignored a lot of red flags, but Sadie suspected that at the time, it was easy to tell herself they were disconnected events.

"Yeah," Allison gave a brittle laugh. "I'm still coming to that revelation myself. However you feel, believe me when I say it's ten times more terrifying for me. Someone wants to *kill* me. How am I supposed to come to terms with that?"

CHAPTER ELEVEN

"I think I might have to move out of state."

At Allison's words, Sadie exchanged another look with Penny. Her friend looked worried and upset, but also understanding. It *might* be for the best, even if it felt a lot like giving up.

"Let's wait and see how the investigation goes," Sadie suggested. "Maybe we can move the trailer behind the building so it's not so visible. The police *are* working on tracking down the killer. If they figure out who it is and things go back to normal, then there's no reason for you to uproot your entire life."

"You really want me to keep working here after all of this?"

"We can't put our other guests and our clients' dogs at risk," Penny stated firmly before Sadie could speak, "but like Sadie said, if the police arrest the person behind all of this, then the risk is gone. And I know we've had a lot of compliments from clients who have tried your grooming services. I think your grooming business is a great addition."

"This is all very fresh, still," Sadie added. "I don't want to make any lasting decisions right now. We probably aren't going to reopen the motel for another few days, so we don't have to decide what to do this very instant."

Allison nodded, her expression grateful. "Okay." She took a deep breath and rose to her feet. "I'll just have to hope that this creep who's been trying to rip my life to shreds walks into the police station and confesses, because right now, that feels like the only way out of this." She gave a self-deprecating laugh as if she knew how unlikely that was, then added, "I should head home. I don't like being out here, especially not after dark. This entire stretch of road gives me the heebie-jeebies, after what happened. But I do feel lighter after this talk. I just wish I'd seen the warning signs before someone died."

"Yeah," Sadie said softly. She couldn't imagine the guilt Allison must be feeling. "Just take the next couple of days to—"

She broke off, nearly jumping out of her skin

when the lobby's door handle jiggled. They had forgotten to lock it when Allison came in, and the door swung open, revealing a fluffy white dog with a permanent grin on her face and behind her, Georgia McKinney, who peered around the room and gave a delighted smile that matched her dog's when she saw Allison. Jasper got up and trotted over to them, his tail wagging. Sadie caught his collar on his way past; he was friendly, but she didn't know if Kiana would appreciate him rushing into her space.

"I *thought* I recognized your car," she said, her voice too cheerful and loud in contrast to the somber conversation that had just ended. "I wanted to see if I could reschedule Kiana's appointment, and while I'm at it, pick up some of that dog-safe sunscreen for her nose. We ran out last week, and she has a sunburn already."

Georgia and Kiana stepped the rest of the way into the lobby, letting the door swing shut behind them. Kiana tugged on her leash toward Allison, who dropped into a crouch to greet the dog automatically. It was clear Kiana knew her well — she seemed thrilled to see her groomer.

Sadie glanced around. None of them had even noticed Georgia park, and the woman's sudden, jarring appearance seemed to have left them all stunned. Georgia took full advantage of their silence to continue talking.

"I also wanted to apologize for canceling my appointment at the last minute on Saturday. I saw my ex-husband hanging around in the parking lot and decided to nope right out of there. What would be a good day for you? I could do Saturday again, or Thursday afternoon if you have any available appointments sooner."

"Um, I'm not really taking appointments right now," Allison said, recovering. She stood up and brushed dog fur off of her pants — there was a lot of it. Kiana was shedding profusely.

They all stared as a clump of fur drifted to the floor. Kiana sniffed it, then shook, shedding more white fluffy fur like rain.

"Are you sure?" Georgia said. "She really needs it, and I just don't have the equipment to groom her properly at home. She'll feel so much better in the summer heat with a thorough grooming. You know how she gets in the summer. She's been suffering terribly, and I just don't feel safe taking her to another groomer. I know *you'll* treat her right, and she always loves seeing you."

Allison winced. Sadie saw her common sense warring with the need to help a dog that clearly needed it. The dog groomer turned to face her almost reluctantly, not even needing to talk for Sadie to understand that she wanted to know if she could schedule just this one appointment.

"We could help you move the grooming supplies back inside," Sadie offered. "You could groom Kiana in the kennel room. If we move your trailer out of sight behind the building, no one would even know you're here."

"Oh, that would be just great!" Georgia said. "I'll pay extra if you need me to. And don't forget that sunscreen — do you have any on hand right now? We were hoping to go on a hike to that river she loves tomorrow, but the best spot is sunny, and her nose is so sensitive…"

"I've got some in the grooming trailer," Allison said. "I'll go get it. Um, I hate to ask, but could one of you schedule her? I'm linked to my old client notes with the system here, so you should have all of Kiana's information on file."

"Yeah, I'll do it," Sadie said. She sat down behind the front desk as Allison left the lobby. She turned to Georgia, a customer service smile settling automatically onto her face.

"All right, what was your last name again?"

"It's McKinney," Georgia said. She spelled it for

Sadie, who typed it in, but the client notes didn't pop up. She tried Kiana's name and then Kiana's name with Georgia's last name, but that didn't bring anything up either.

"I'm sorry. I know she said she linked her notes, but I'm just not seeing anything."

"Um, you might want to try my married name. I might not have remembered to ask her to change it after the divorce. It would be under Derry." Sadie began to type "Georgia Derry," but her fingers paused on the keyboard.

Derry. Like Jake Derry. Jake, who had been lurking around the motel that Saturday, right around when Georgia said she had spotted her ex-husband.

The same ex-husband whose affair Allison had revealed to his now ex-wife.

CHAPTER TWELVE

"Did you find it?"

Georgia's voice snapped her out of her thoughts. She looked up at the other woman and said, "Georgia, what's your ex-husband's name?"

"Jake," Georgia said. "I don't think the account would be under his name, though. I was almost always the one who handled Kiana's grooming appointments."

"I think I've met him."

Georgia's eyebrows rose. "I *did* see him in the motel's parking lot. Did he ask after me?"

"No." She took a deep breath, her heart racing. "What exactly happened between you two? I'm sorry for asking, but it's important."

"Oh no, it's fine. I'm pretty open about it. He's the one who ought to be embarrassed, not me. He was having an affair with a younger woman who he worked with behind my back for nearly a year. I never suspected a thing until he was running late and asked the woman to pick up 'his dog' from the groomer."

Georgia reached down to pat Kiana's head. The dog gazed up at her adoringly.

"Apparently, his affair partner didn't know he was married. Allison figured out what was going on and warned me about it. She even helped me get the evidence I needed to completely steamroll over him in court." Georgia gave a small, sharp smile. "Honestly, I'm better off without him. Kiana and I do just fine on our own. And I have to admit, it's been satisfying to watch his life fall apart. His girlfriend broke up with him a couple weeks after he moved in with her, he got fired from his job because it went against their work policies for him to be involved with a subordinate, and absolutely none of our friends will talk to him. Even his own family has been giving him the cold shoulder ever since I told them about the affair. Jake wrecked his own life, and as far as I'm concerned, he deserves it."

"How did he handle all of that?" Sadie asked. "Was he angry?"

"Oh, he was livid," Georgia said, smiling. "He even tried to get back together with me once. When I laughed in his face, he lost his temper in a way I'd never seen before. I had to call the police that night, and my brother moved in with me temporarily to make sure I was safe. He's this big ex-military guy I think Jake has always been at least a little afraid of. I haven't heard a peep from him since. I think he finally got the message that night."

Except he hadn't. Sadie could almost see it all falling into place as Georgia spoke. Jake, though clearly an inexperienced camper, had chosen dispersed camping rather than a regular campsite or their motel during most of his visit to Greencreek. She knew dispersed camping was free, and there would be no record of where he was staying. He had been lurking around the motel's parking lot on Saturday, not to see whether he wanted to stay in one of the rooms, but to see the layout and possibly find a good spot to shoot Allison from.

Only, he failed to kill his true target. Had he come to the motel during the rainstorm because he needed shelter, or was he just hoping to get closer to Allison and finish the job? If he couldn't hurt his ex-wife, then he must have turned his rage to the next closest target — the woman who exposed his affair.

And he was out there, right now, in the dark, with Allison.

"Sadie," Penny said. "What is it?"

"We need to warn Allison this instant," Sadie said, shooting to her feet. "Penny, can you call Sheriff Islington? I think I know who killed Barbara, and I think he's going to go after Allison next."

She took her pepper spray from her purse and turned her cellphone's flashlight on, then hurried out of the lobby, letting Penny and Georgia's worried voices fade behind her as she jogged around the corner of the building to where the grooming trailer sat. The door was open, but the interior was dark. Sadie walked up the metal steps, shining her light inside. There was no sign of Allison, but she saw a little tub of sunscreen on its side on the floor, as if someone had dropped it.

She stood in the dark trailer, her heart pounding as she tried to figure out where he would have taken her. Into the woods… or his motel room?

The motel room was closer and would be easier to check. She hurried back to the lobby, shoving the door open and pushing past Penny to get the master key out of the locked drawer under the register.

"Sheriff Islington's on the phone right now," Penny said. "What's going on, Sadie?"

"He has her," Sadie said, her hands shaking. She shoved her phone at Penny, who took it with her free hand — the other one was clutching her own phone to her ear. "In case we need a light. Hurry."

Penny followed her outside, Georgia and Kiana trailing behind, confused. Jasper had slipped outside with them and quickly caught up to Sadie as she raced down the walkway to Room Nine. The curtains were drawn, but she could see the dim glow of a light inside. She didn't hesitate. She shoved the key into the lock and turned, pushing the door open in the same motion.

She saw Allison first. The woman was tied to the rolling desk chair, which had been moved to the middle of the room. She was gagged with a strip of twisted up fabric – it looked like it had been cut from the motel's sheet set. Her eyes were terrified.

The next thing she saw was Jake holding a rifle, which was aimed right at Allison's chest. It had a scope on it, but this close, he wasn't bothering to look through it.

Jasper pushed his head past Sadie's legs and let out a low growl, a sound she had only heard him make once before in her life. In the same moment, Jake swung the rifle toward them.

Sadie screamed, raised her pepper spray, and fired a stream right into his eyes.

The gun went off and she felt bits of drywall crumble from the ceiling, but that was the only wild shot he managed to get off. He dropped the gun and shouted as he rubbed his eyes frantically. Sadie rushed into the room and kicked the gun under the bed. Jake stumbled into her, but he wasn't attacking her he was trying to make his way to the bathroom so he could rinse his eyes out under the faucet.

Sadie turned to ask for help, but Penny was already there, rushing forward to grab the chair Allison was tied to and help her roll it out of the room. Georgia's hands were full with Kiana's leash and Jasper's collar – she'd had the presence of mind to pull him back when everything broke out into chaos.

Sadie shut the motel room's door behind her, hoping it would delay Jake for even a few moments, and they pushed Allison along the bumpy sidewalk and back to the lobby as quickly as they could. Once they were all inside, they locked the door and began searching for something to cut Allison free from her ties. Sadie felt a rush of gratitude for the cinder block walls and heavy, metal door.

They still fell silent when Jake pounded on that door, shouting something unintelligible at them through the thick walls, but he fell silent as soon as he heard the approaching sirens. The four of them waited until Sheriff Islington came to give them the all-clear.

EPILOGUE

The feeling of having welcomed Barbara's killer under her roof left Sadie off kilter for days, but at least she had the satisfaction of watching Jake Derry be taken away in handcuffs that night, his eyes still swollen and puffy from the pepper spray.

It was a long night. Sadie spent most of it comforting Allison with Penny. The other woman was beside herself and didn't seem capable of making the drive home by herself. She didn't want to be alone either, so they put her up in one of their motel rooms for the night.

Georgia was the first one the police allowed to leave. She murmured a quiet "I'll call back later this week to schedule something" to Sadie as she went by, and let Kiana give Allison a kiss on the cheek before she got into her car. Jasper stayed close to Sadie as the police milled around them. He seemed unusually on edge, and she patted his shoulder fondly, surprised and a little pleased that he had it in him to growl at someone who was threatening them.

Sam showed up just as Georgia left. She told him what happened, and felt a pang of guilt for the panic and worry she felt in him as he pulled her into a tight hug. Maybe this relationship wasn't good for him. She just couldn't seem to stop finding herself elbow-deep in trouble, and each time he acted like he had almost lost something precious.

Their little group recovered slowly, but recover they did. Allison came back on Thursday with a vengeance, a paintbrush, and multiple cans of colored paint in hand. She singled Penny out and pointed dramatically at her grooming trailer.

"It's over now. I don't have to live in fear anymore, which means I can do whatever I want to my trailer without worrying about it catching the wrong eye. You're good at drawing, right? Will you help me?"

Sadie couldn't draw to save her life, but she helped by making some lemonade out of a powder mix —she didn't have the time or the desire to squeeze twenty lemons by hand, nor the lemons —

and sat on a folding chair in the shade. Jasper bounded through the tall grass behind her as she watched the other two women paint Allison's new logo. It was a beautiful day, especially with the faint breeze that had picked up. She smacked a mosquito when it landed on her knee, but that was just part and parcel of living in Georgia. She could hear Cody training Angus in the grassy field behind the building and the growl of Sam's lawnmower as he mowed his yard on the other side of the tree line.

The storm had passed and life was beginning to look bright again.

Printed in Dunstable, United Kingdom